AMMANANNA

AKSHAY AKULA

To amma and nanna

Contents

Foreword

There are people in this world whose presence leaves a quiet but lasting imprint on everyone they meet. My mother and father were those kinds of people. They didn't seek attention, nor did they live their lives for recognition—but the impact they had was profound, shaping not only my life but the lives of many around them.

This book is a tribute to who they were—not just as parents, but as individuals, partners, and human beings navigating life with grace, strength, and love.

Through these pages, I invite you to meet them the way I knew them: in the little details of everyday life, in the hard-earned wisdom passed down over time, in the way they loved without condition.

Their story is not a grand epic filled with fame or fanfare. It's something more powerful—it's the story of how ordinary people create extraordinary legacies through kindness, courage, and compassion.

Whether you read this as someone who knew them, or as someone discovering them for the first time, I hope you'll see what I saw: two lives beautifully lived, and deeply loved.

Preface

This book is not meant to be a biography, nor is it a complete history. It is a mosaic of memories, reflections, and moments — pieced together from stories I was told, experiences I lived, and emotions I continue to carry.

My goal was not to tell a perfect tale, but an honest one.

Some chapters are joyful, filled with laughter and light. Others are quiet and heavy, shaped by time and loss. But through it all, one truth remains: my parents lived with love, and that love echoed into everything they touched.

I hope this book serves as a reminder — for me, for those who knew them, and for those who read these pages — that ordinary lives can leave extraordinary legacies.

Thank you for taking the time to read their story.

Acknowledgements

This book would not exist without the love, support, and encouragement of many people.

To my family — thank you for sharing your memories, your stories, and your patience as I pieced this together one page at a time.

To my friends — your encouragement, kind words, and occasional tough love kept me going during the moments when I doubted myself.(especially to my friend Jilla shrikanta)

To those who read early drafts and offered your feedback, thank you for helping me find the heart of this book.

To the quiet hours, the old photographs, the handwritten notes, and the long walks filled with thought — you gave me the space to reflect and remember.

And most of all, to my parents — your lives inspired these pages, and your love lives on in every word.

PROLOGUE

I was sitting alone one afternoon, flipping through an old photo album. The corners were worn, the pages curled with age, and yet each picture pulled me back in time like it had just been taken.

I saw smiles I hadn't seen in years, moments I thought I had forgotten, and behind every image was a story. A story of love, of sacrifice, of two people who shaped not just my life, but the way I see the world.

That's when I knew I had to write this book.

Not to capture every detail perfectly, because memories are never perfect. But to honor the people who raised me, who loved deeply, and who left behind more than they ever realized.

This is their story — and in many ways, it's mine too.

I

Childhood and early years

My mother was born into a family where there was enough to eat and drink. She has three brothers—two elder brothers and one younger. Even though she is the third child, her parents gave her more freedom than her three brothers. She used to eat mud but a lot.

My mother eating mud.

Her parents never beat her but would scold her when she ate mud. She was a naughty girl and a kho kho player, and she liked yellow papads, which was famous in those days. She never argued with her parents and had many friends. But her mother never allowed her to go out.

My maternal grandmother used to go to the farm for work. My mother would look after her brothers even though she was younger than them. She used to cook food. One day, her mother went to work as usual. Her grandmother was at home, and my mother and her cousin sister were also there. Both of them were in 5th grade, but they used to do many things that were not related to their age. They cooked food in a big matka, like biryani making pot(handi). No one helped them, but they successfully completed the task.

My mother kneading dough.

My mother never asked her parents for anything for her needs and wishes, but they always got her everything she needed. One day, my grandmother assigned some work to my mother, but she failed to complete it. My maternal grandmother got angry and caught her hair for the first time. At that moment, my grandmother's father stopped her. He loved my mother more than my grandmother.

So, my mother had a joyful childhood.

II

How they met and early life together

One fine day, after my mother completed her tenth board exams, a marriage proposal came through one of her father's friends. However, my grandmother initially rejected it. Surprisingly, the very next day, the groom himself came directly to my maternal grandparents and spoke to them about the proposal—and this time, they accepted. The wedding was finalized and took place on 26-04-2000.

The marriage was made grand and beautiful by my mother's brothers. However, due to a significant age difference between my parents, they found it difficult to bond in the initial months of marriage. Over time, my mother slowly began to mingle with her new family. She started thinking deeply about her responsibilities and tried to build a bond with her in-laws. My paternal grandmother was a bit harsh toward her in the beginning, but my mother never took it to heart. Instead, she responded with love and kindness, even when she wasn't fully understood by her new family.

Years passed, and eventually, my paternal grandparents began to understand and appreciate my mother. My father, on the other hand, was a nature lover whose dream was to travel the entire globe. During the early years of their marriage, he was frequently out of state, often leaving my mother alone at home while he went on tours with his friends. In the span of 17 years, he traveled across India and to neighboring countries—but he went alone with his friends , without my mother.

My father also had the habit of spending his earnings freely, especially on real estate and enjoyment. But after many years, one day, my mother had an open and honest conversation with him. From that day forward, he began to include her in his travels. They grew closer, shared real love, and truly began to understand each other. Gradually, he also learned to use money more wisely.

We are a joint family, and although my parents had many disagreements—mostly misunderstandings rather than fights—they always resolved them with patience and love. This is how they built a strong and lasting relationship. Through it all, they remained happy, supportive, and deeply connected.

Watching my parents talking happily.

III
Parenthood

The biggest challenge for my parents came when we—my sister and I—were born. Although we came into their lives a bit late, we quickly became aware of the world around us. My mother, despite all the responsibilities on her shoulders, took care of both of us and the entire extended family. Ours is a large, joint family, and in those early days, ours was the only house in the area. After 6 p.m., the surroundings would fall completely silent, and going out at night was nothing less than an adventure—filled with the danger of snakes, thieves, and complete darkness.

Despite not being a pet lover, my mother lovingly cared for our dog, Rocky. She faced many difficulties during those times, but she overcame them all with quiet strength and determination. She never taught me anything wrong—only kindness, resilience, and courage. She was always there through both my failures and my successes. She stood beside me like a shield, while my father was the backbone of our family.

My mom feeding rocky.

My father is my hero. He taught me how to walk, how to run, and he filled my childhood with joy and love. He bought me a whole store of toys, and one day when I asked him for a bicycle, he didn't hesitate—he bought it for me immediately. He was strict only about two things: eating well and sports. He even hired a coach for me to train in badminton, and I went on to play at the state level.

He also ensured I studied at the best school, just as he had planned for me. In my entire life, he has only ever slapped me once, when I was in the 5th class—and after that, never again. Both my parents believed in exposing us to the world at a young age. They took us on trips and tours early in life, which helped me gain confidence and awareness.

One moment I'll never forget is when I was 11 years old. I was terrified of water. When we went to Lakshadweep as a family, my father gently pushed me into the shallow sea—not to scare me, but to help me conquer that fear. From that moment, I was never afraid of water again.

Another memory that stays with me is our family trip to Araku(AndhraPradesh,India) when I was in 4th class. It was a hill station, and we went along with my maternal grandparents and extended family. As we drove up the hills, everyone in the vehicle started to feel breathless due to the altitude. The moment we reached the top, we rushed to a nearby resort to rest and freshen up. Later, my father and I went for a walk in the chilly, snowy weather. Along the way, I spotted a horse and immediately asked my father if I could ride it. Without hesitation, he called over the handler and helped me climb on. I rode the horse in that cold, thin-air atmosphere—something no one expected from me. My family was shocked and proud. My mother, standing at a distance, encouraged me with a smile. That experience was only possible because my father was by my side, and my mother was behind me with unwavering support.

To me, my parents are nothing short of gods. Our family holds deep faith in God, especially in our Kula Daivam, Komuravelli Mallanna Swamy(god). We follow traditions passed down from our great-great-grandparents, including a grand pooja called Patnalu, which we conduct once every three years. It's a major ritual that requires days of preparation, spiritual dedication, and immense physical energy. As the first daughter-in-law of our paternal house, my mother plays a central role in this tradition. Despite the workload and pressure, she always rose to the occasion with grace.

She faced many hardships while raising us, especially in the early days. I remember one touching incident—my mother once took me to a family function when I was still a toddler. I was wearing a diaper, and at some point during the event, I soiled it. We were far from home, and she had heavy jewelry on, but without any hesitation, she rushed me to the restroom and cleaned me up with love and care.

This is how Amma raised me—with strength, selflessness, and an endless amount of love.

IV
Overcoming Obstacles

During the COVID-19 pandemic, my mother was affected by the virus. It was one of the toughest times for our family. My sister and I were sent to stay with our maternal grandparents for safety, while my paternal grandparents stayed back to support my mother. She was isolated in a room, and the only person who stayed with her was my father.

My parents during COVID-19 pandemic.

Eventually, my father also tested positive for COVID. They were the only two in that room for a long time. Every day, my paternal grandparents would prepare food and leave it near the door. Once my grandmother left, my father would open the door and collect the meals. That's how they managed and survived those long five months of isolation.

Despite being unwell, my father remained strong and supportive. He took care of my mother completely—feeding her, placing wet cloths on her forehead to reduce her fever, and doing whatever was needed to make her feel better.

They didn't waste those five months; instead, they spent time watching Ramayana and Mahabharata on TV, sharing stories from their childhood, and reminiscing about their wedding and early days of marriage.

Even though both of them were affected by the virus, they stood by each other and came out of it stronger than ever. That period deepened their bond and helped build an unbreakable relationship. It wasn't just my father and grandparents who stepped in during that difficult time—my mother's elder brother stay's in karimnagar(telangana) also showed immense love and support.

Her big brother left his own family and traveled to Mancherial just to see her. He didn't care about the risk to his health or the distance—he simply wanted to be with his sister. He stayed with her during her illness, and it was then that my mother truly realized the strength and depth of the bond between a brother and sister. Unfortunately, after he returned home, he too contracted COVID—but thankfully, he recovered quickly. That experience brought our bond with my uncle even closer.

Later, there was a small clash within our joint family, which led to my mother moving out of the house for a while. However, after nearly two years, all the misunderstandings were resolved, and today, our family stands united again. This is how my parents faced and overcame every difficulty that life threw at them—together.

In my life, my parents have never forced me to do anything. Every decision I made was based on my own interest. After my tenth board exams, I asked my father what stream I should choose, and he simply said, "Take whatever you want." I chose the CEC (Commerce, Economics, Civics) group purely out of interest, and both of them supported me wholeheartedly.

My parents were never strict—except for two things. My father was always particular about food and sports. He believed in discipline in those areas, but for everything else, he gave me full freedom. He always says, "Work hard now and enjoy the rest of your life."

My mother just wants me to be happy while I study—she never wants me to feel pressured or sad. They admitted me to a hostel when I was just 13 years old, not out of necessity but because they believed it would help me study better. I was okay with that decision, even though the first two years were difficult for me health-wise.

The hostel was in Hyderabad, around four hours from our hometown. Whenever I called my parents—even if I didn't ask them to—they would come to see me immediately, without delay. Despite the heavy cost of my education—my school fees alone were ₹5 lakhs—my father still invested another ₹3 lakhs on me. That's the kind of love and support they've given me throughout my life.

V
Memorable moments

One day, our entire family, along with some close family friends, went on a trip to a hill station. On the way, we got stuck in a heavy traffic jam. In an attempt to avoid the congestion, our driver tried to take a side route. But unexpectedly, a police officer threw a stone toward our vehicle. The stone hit our car with force, startling all of us. Fortunately, nothing happened to my sister who was seated near the window where the stone struck.

Immediately, my father and his friends got down from the car and confronted the policeman who had thrown the stone. Without hesitation, my father went up to him and slapped him. The impact caused the officer's nose to bleed, but surprisingly, the policeman didn't say a word in return. Instead, he silently cleared the road for us and let our vehicle pass. That moment left a strong impression on me. It was then that I truly understood how much courage my father had and how fiercely he protected his family. That day, I saw the depth of his love and care.

My father never sat with me to teach academics, but he taught me something far more valuable—how to be a good human being. He always told me to help others, never to cause trouble, and to make sure that no one suffers because of us. One of the most important values he instilled in me was this: "No one should go hungry because of our actions."

CONCLUSION

Through every season of life—be it love, hardship, conflict, or celebration—my parents have stood as living examples of strength, sacrifice, and unshakable love. Their journey was never perfect, but it was real. From a simple wedding rooted in tradition to years of adjustment, from miscommunications to deep understanding, from personal dreams to shared sacrifices—they built a bond that didn't just survive life's storms, but grew stronger through them.

They faced family challenges, financial uncertainties, health crises, and even a global pandemic, but never let go of each other's hands. My father, with his quiet determination and fearless protection, and my mother, with her boundless love and patience, have shown me what it means to be selfless, brave, and compassionate.

They never forced me down a path but instead let me shape my own, guiding me with trust and love. They taught me values not from textbooks, but through the life they lived—honesty, kindness, courage, and the importance of staying grounded, no matter how high we soar.

This book isn't just a tribute—it is a mirror of everything they are and everything they have given me. Their story is the root from which I grow, and no matter how far life takes me, I will always carry them in every heartbeat, every memory, and every dream I chase.

MY FINAL WORDS

As I bring this journey to a close, I find myself overwhelmed with gratitude—for the life I've been given, the lessons I've learned, and the parents who made all of it possible.

Writing this story has not just been a way to honor my mother and father, but a way to rediscover them. Through each memory, I saw them not only as parents, but as individuals—people who laughed, cried, struggled, sacrificed, and loved with all their hearts. They were not perfect, and that's what made their story even more beautiful. It was real. It was human. It was full of courage and grace.

My father, with his boldness, his dreams, and his unwavering willpower, taught me to never fear the world and to protect those you love at any cost. He showed me what strength looks like—not just in his hands, but in his choices.

My mother, with her endless patience, silent endurance, and gentle heart, taught me what unconditional love means. She carried burdens silently, wore a smile even through her pain, and raised us with values that shaped who we are today.

Together, they are my foundation. Every time life knocks me down, I remember their resilience. Every time I'm unsure, I hear their words echo in my heart. They gave me not just life, but a reason to live with purpose.

This story is a piece of their legacy. But more importantly, it's a reminder—to myself and to everyone who reads it—that behind every strong child stands a pair of silent warriors who gave everything, often without asking for anything in return.

If there's one thing I hope you carry from this book, it's this: cherish your parents, listen to their stories, hold onto the lessons they quietly teach you, and never forget the love that shaped you.

In the end, we all return to our roots—and mine will always lead me home to them.

This journey never ends and continues to be further parts.

www.ingramcontent.com/pod-product-compliance
Lightning Source LLC
Chambersburg PA
CBHW020519160726
47991CB00007B/3035